FOSTERCARE FEELINGS

```
            J X X H G
          J F E E L I N G S
        A E O W E S N E T A T
        A N A N O I T C E J E R D
        O D K N A S A D N E S S C
    K Z E M Y G W A T R D D R W U
    G N T T E N E U E G A R T U O
    P U S R A N A R C S U G X I X
    Q O U S A T V P H A W N E F U
    C T A I G E B Y P E F N Z F C
    L H N A M F E U O Z B M Q
    S X E R A C R E T S O F Q
        E X M Y B B A R C S K
          V E D E V F I T
            G J P O A
```

WORD BANK

ANGER	EXHAUSTED	FOSTERCARE	REJECTION
CRABBY	FEAR	OUTRAGE	SADNESS
ENVY	FEELINGS	RAGE	TENSE

What Feeling is this _____?

DRAW A PICTURE OR WRITE ABOUT A TIME WHEN YOU ARE HAPPY

SELFCARE MUSIC

WHEN DO YOU LISTEN TO MUSIC?

DRAW
SELFCARE

WHEN DO YOU DRAW?

TAKE A NAP

HOW IS TAKING A NAP HELPFUL TO YOU?

MATCHING

Match the word on the left side to its PICTURE on the right side.

1. ____ FEAR

2. ____ OUTRAGE

3. ____ SADNESS

4. ____ TENSE

5. ____ ENVY

6. ____ RAGE

7. ____ CRABBY

8. ____ ANGER

9. ____ REJECTION

10. ____ EXHAUSTED

A.
B.
C.
D.
E.
F.
G.
H.
I.
J.

DO YOU FEEL FOSTERCARE FEELINGS? IF SO, WHEN?

WHAT FEELING DO YOU FEEL ON
MONDAY?

CRABBY
ANGER
REJECTION
EXHAUSTED

WHAT FEELING DO YOU FEEL ON TUESDAY?

I-STATEMENTS

I - STATEMENTS "I" statement is a style of communication that focuses on the feelings or beliefs of YOU rather than thoughts and feelings that YOU think the listener feels.

> FILL IN THE BLANK WITH YOUR OWN WORDS - Example: "I" statement response: "I feel very sad when I hear rude words because they hurt my feelings. I like playing with people who use nice words."

I FEEL _____

WHEN _____

BECAUSE _____

WHAT I NEED IS _____

I FEEL _____

WHEN _____

BECAUSE _____

WHAT I NEED IS _____

PLAY BALL

SELFCARE

WHAT FEELING DO YOU FEEL ON WEDNESDAY?

WHAT FEELING DO YOU FEEL ON
THURSDAY?

Body Map
TRY ADDING WHAT FEELING YOU FEEL IN YOUR BODY ON THE BODY

TRY ADDING YOUR OWN!

WHAT FEELING DO YOU FEEL ON

FRIDAY?

WHAT FEELING DO YOU FEEL MOST?

What Feeling is this _____?

Coloring Page

SELFCARE

WHAT ARE YOU FEELING TODAY?

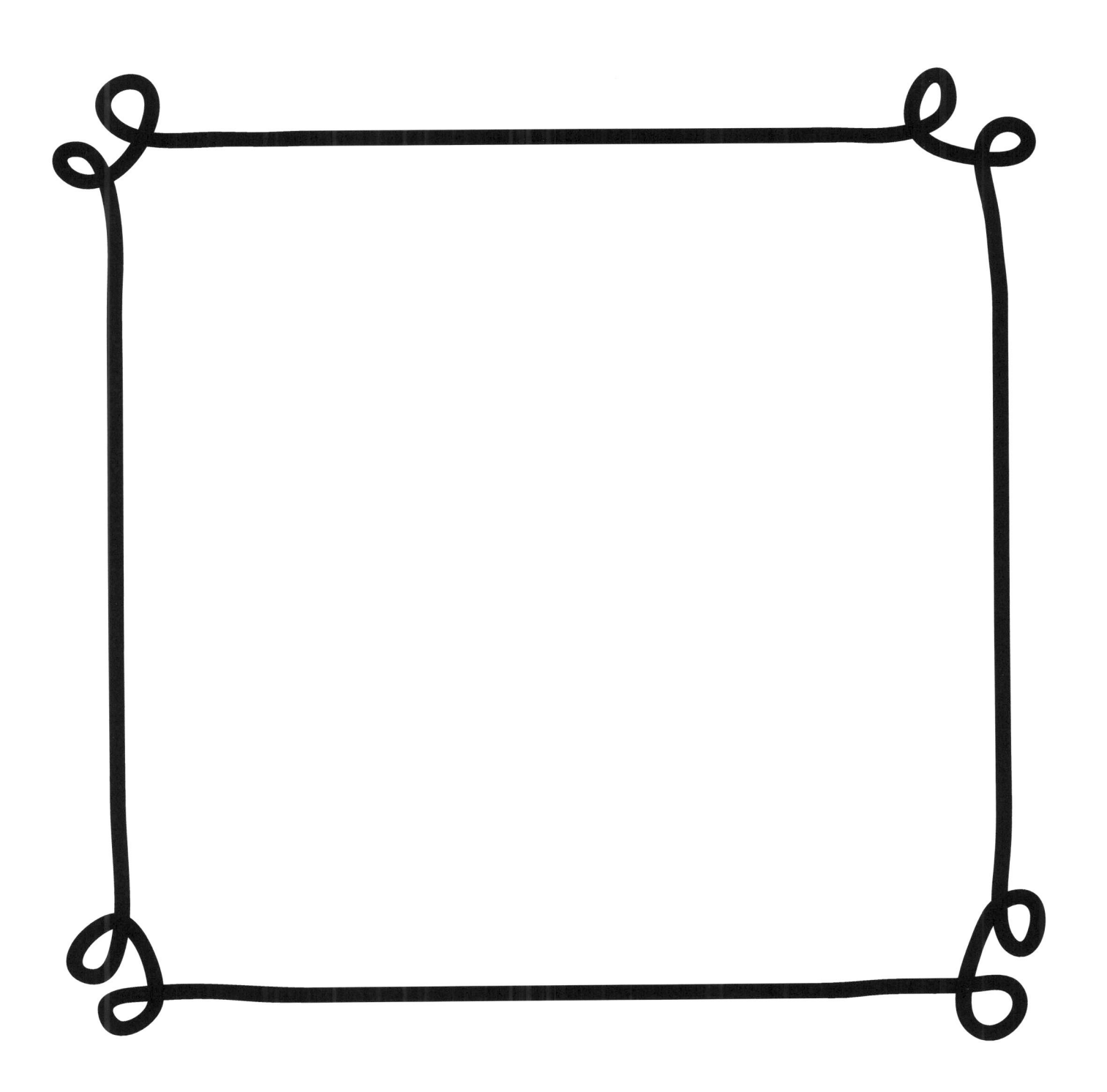

What Feeling is this _____?

READING

SELFCARE

What Feeling is this _____?

WHAT ARE YOU FEELING TODAY?

FEAR
OUTRAGE
SADNESS
TENSE
ENVY
RAGE

Coloring Page

SELFCARE

WHAT ARE YOU FEELING TODAY?

SELFCARE

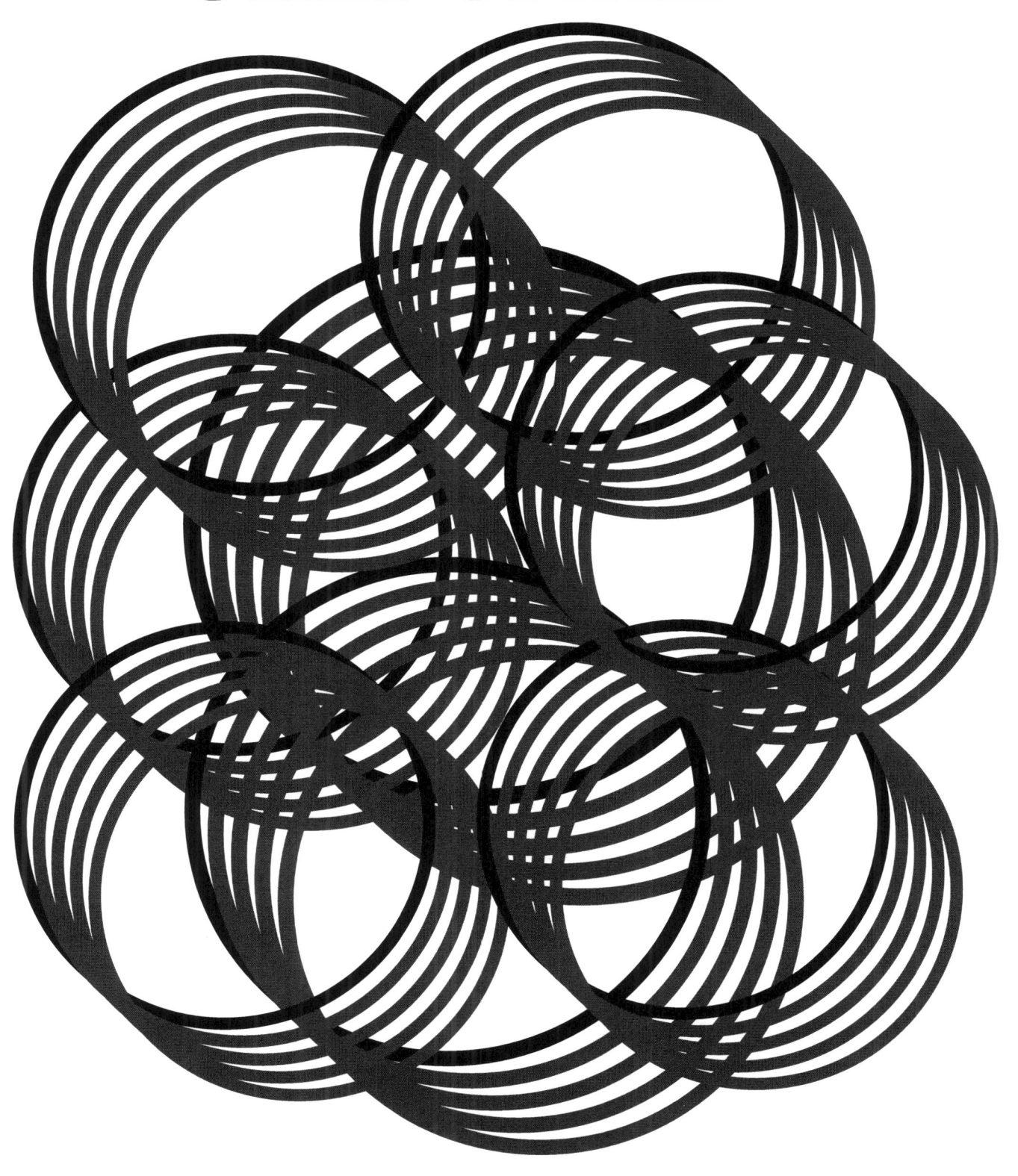

FOOD!!!

SELFCARE

WHAT ARE YOU FEELING TODAY?

STRESS JAR

HOW A GLITTER JAR CAN HELP KIDS CONTROL THEIR FEELINGS

When kids are stressed, sad, or angry, the amygdala's natural fight, flight, or freeze response kicks in, making rational decision-making nearly impossible.

Mindfulness gives kids space and time to calm down and pay attention to what is going on in their body and environment. Regularly practicing mindfulness reduces stress and increases wellness and self-control.

Glitter jars are a useful mindfulness tool at home and school. Watching the glitter swirl to the bottom of the jar gives kids time to calm down and regain control.

Instructions

Pour 1/2 cup of distilled warm water into the jar.
Pour 1/2 cup of glitter glue or clear glue into the jar.
Add 1-2 teaspoons of extra glitter, beads or buttons to the jar.
Fill up the remainder of the jar with warm distilled water.
If desired, use a hot glue gun to squeeze a ring of glue around the lid of the jar.
You can also use small plastic jars from dollar store.

Printed in Great Britain
by Amazon